D1082768

LOVE IS LOVE

LOVE AROUND THE WORLD, VOL. II

FLEUR PIERETS

Illustrated by
FATINHA RAMOS

SIXFOOTPRESS
Houston

We are Fleur and Julian, and we are two women in love. 13 is the number of countries where we have gotten married. 13 times we said "I do!" We travel around the world to talk about marriage, to let people know it is an act of love between any two people, not just between a man and a woman.

Our love is about looking in the same direction and making the world a better place. So after 13 countries, we are going to 15 more!

Julian and I absolutely love sunshine and dancing. We found a perfect combination of the two in **Colombia**, where marriage celebrations last all night. We danced until we saw the sun come up over the green hills of an eternal spring.

The rights of LGBTQ+ persons in Denmark are some of the most extensive in the world. For the Danish, weddings are a celebration and recognition of love. Whether girls marry boys, girls marry girls, or boys marry boys, in Denmark, no one can tell you what not to do.

Sometimes I ask Julian, "Do you still love me enough to keep going?"
But our love is bigger than the sun and the moon and the sea and the stars.
So if all of the 195 countries in the world allow us to get married, we will
say "I do" in each and every one of them. We got into the van and drove
to the next country on the list: **Austria**.

Berlin, the capital of **Germany**, is known as one of the most open and accepting cities in the world. A total of 2,540 same-sex marriages were celebrated in the first year that the law was officially adopted. Who do you think one of those couples was? Us!

Two women traveling the world to get married in every country that allows them? Even after wedding number 17, it is big news! So when we arrive in **Luxembourg**, there are cameras and microphones everywhere! And we enjoy talking about our trip and how much we love each other.

Julian and I love the idea of getting married in the traditional wedding attire of each country we visit. In **Norway**, the traditional wedding costume is called a bunad. Few Norwegians still use the headdresses, but I want to try it out. Don't you think it looks great?

Taiwan is the only country in Asia where we can get married. The country's road to LGBTQ+ equality started with Chi Chia-Wei, an activist who has fought for marriage equality since he was 17 years old. The law was finally approved in 2017, when he was 59 years old. "I waited for this day for 41 years, 6 months, and 24 days," Chi tells us.

Finding the perfect location in **Malta** isn't easy. Whether you want to get married in the original home of the Knights of Malta, in the proximity of the Blue Lagoon, or in the secret coves, every spot is as beautiful as the next.

Discrimination regarding sexual orientation and expression has been banned in **New Zealand** since 1993. They understand that Julian and I are two grownups who are very much in love with each other, and that we have decided to make a lifelong commitment to one another.

Julian and I often say things like "23 countries down, 172 to go!" while we hope for more countries to join the list while we are traveling. But first we go to **Argentina** and get married in the Valley of the Moon. Just because we love the name.

In London, in the **United Kingdom**, we talk to children in many schools about bullying. It is something that no child should ever experience because it hurts too much. Luckily all the kids understand and make a promise to take care of each other.

If a person in **Sweden** feels they have been discriminated against, they can turn to a government agency called the Equality Ombudsman. The law is clear that discrimination is not acceptable. No wonder both Julian and I were eager to get to meet the people from this wonderful country!

Many people say that **Uruguay** is the most LGBT-friendly country in Latin America. Therefore we thought it was a good idea to marry during the Montevideo Pride parade and celebrate our wedding with 120,000 people.

Julian and I love fashion. We are always looking for a local fashion designer in the country where we are getting married. In **South Africa**, we are privileged to go the studio of Palesa Mokubung and choose outfits that give our wedding that extra festive style!

Our wedding adventure ends for the moment in **Ecuador**, the most recent country to legalize same-sex marriage, in 2019. Julian is very proud when she takes me to the altar. We can never stop fighting for things to get better.

Julian and I have now gotten married in 28 countries! We hope we can get married in the next 167 because love is love. As you have learned, love can come in many forms. How amazing it would be if we could keep on traveling from one country to another until we have visited all 195!

Photo: Duncan de Fey

FLEUR PIERETS is an artist, writer, and speaker who focuses on gay identity and positive activism. She is the author of the best-selling book *Julian* and the children's book *Love Around the World*, an American Library Association Rainbow Book List selection.

Together with her late wife, Julian P. Boom, she founded *Et Alors?* magazine. It features conversations with queer musicians, visual artists, writers and performers by whom they are inspired, capturing a world striving for change and awareness of gay imagery and female representation in art history. In 2017, Fleur and Julian started 22–The Project, a performance art piece in which the couple would marry in every country that legalized same-sex marriage. There were 22 countries when they launched the project in 2017; since then, the number of countries has grown to 28.

After wedding #4, in France, Julian was diagnosed with brain cancer. She died shortly thereafter. With this book series, Fleur is seeing their project through to the end.

www.etalorsmagazine.com
www.jfpierets.com
www.22theproject.com